I am an ARO PUBLISHING THIRTY WORD BOOK
My thirty words are:

a	ground	money
am	grin	my
by	he (he's)	pound
chest	hear	see
come (comes)	heart	start
Doctor	heavy	tall
done	how	test
for	I	the
from	makes	tongue
funny	me	with

ISBN 0-89868-187-1 — Library Bound
ISBM 0-89868-188-X — Soft Bound

My First
Doctor Visit

Story by Julia Allen
Pictures by Bob Reese

ARO PUBLISHING

Come see

the Doctor with me!

See how tall

from the ground.

See how heavy

by the pound.

The Doctor comes in

with a grin.

For a start,

he hears my heart.

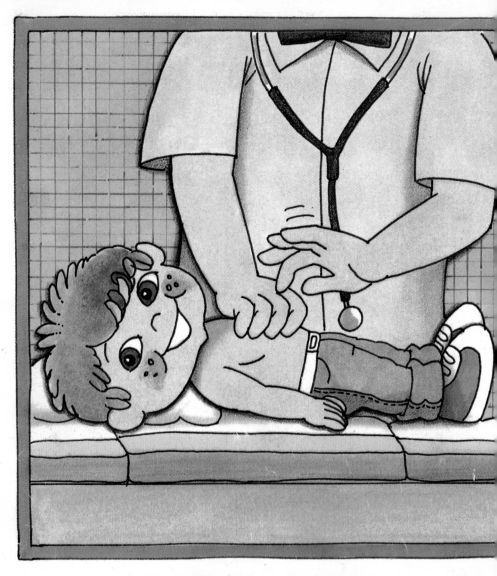

For a test,

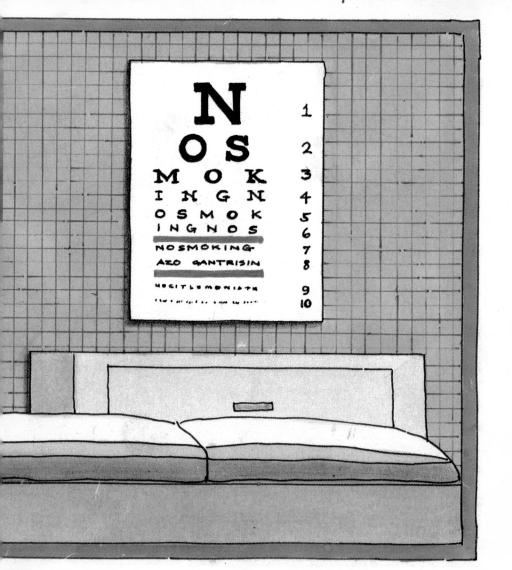

he hears my chest.

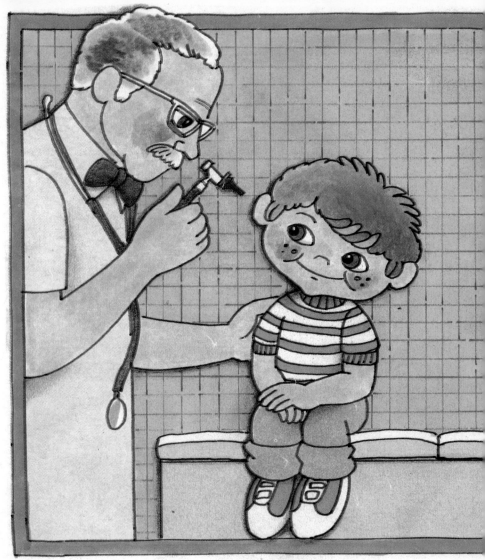

How I hear,

how I see,

makes the Doctor

grin with me.

See my tongue.

I am done.

He's funny

how he makes money.